A DIFFERENT BALL GAME

by Osmond Molarsky
illustrated by James Zingarelli

Coward, McCann & Geoghegan, Inc.
New York

Text copyright © 1979 by Osmond Molarsky
Illustrations copyright © 1979 by James
Zingarelli

Library of Congress Cataloging in Publication
Data
Molarsky, Osmond.
    A different ball game.
    SUMMARY: A soccer enthusiast helps a young
Chilean boy, living in the United States with his
aunt, understand what it means to be arrested
and falsely accused of a crime.
    [1. Juvenile delinquency—Fiction. 2. Soccer—
Fiction] I. Zingarelli, James. II. Title.
PZ7.M7317Di   [Fic]   78-23793
ISBN 0-698-20475-1

Printed in the United States of America

It was Saturday morning, and a few boys were shooting baskets in the school play yard with an old tennis ball they had found. Manolo Blanco was bouncing shots off his foot and through the hoop. His feet could make any kind of ball do almost as much as his hands could, for he had lived most of his life in Chile, where kids play soccer more than all other games put together.

He would still be there, but six months before, Manolo's father and mother and big brother had been arrested and taken away for speaking out against the government. Many people had been sent to prison and put in concentration camps for saying what they thought. Since Manolo was only eleven, the police had let friends send him to his Aunt Carola, who lived in California. He wrote a letter to his parents every week, but he had

3

received only three replies. In each letter his parents said that they were all right and that he should not worry, that they loved him, and that he should be good and not cause trouble for his aunt.

"They write as often as they are permitted," his aunt told him. "They do not forget you." She spoke to him in English most of the time, so he would learn faster.

The only thing Manolo missed more than his parents and his brother was playing soccer with his school team, the Lobos. He played baseball with the Little League, but it wasn't as much fun. The nearest thing to soccer that he had seen in the United States was when a mob of little kids would kick a ball around at recess. They called it kickball, but they used their hands almost as much as their feet.

Manolo's own feet never stopped behaving as if they were at home in Chile. They kicked at almost everything in sight—tin cans, stones, milk cartons, paper cups, candy wrappers, sometimes nothing at all—just an imaginary soccer ball rolling in their direction. Right now, it was an old tennis ball.

The day was very warm for shooting baskets, and by eleven o'clock everyone was very thirsty. When they found that the drinking fountain was turned off, Bill Spender said, "Let's get a drink inside."

"How can we get in?"

"I can get in," Bill said. In less than five minutes he had pried open a window, crawled in, and opened a side door. "This way in!" he called. Soon all were inside drinking their fill.

"We ought to get out of here," Manolo said when he had finished drinking. Everyone else had finished, but no one had moved toward the door.

"What's your hurry? Nobody knows we're here. Let's have some fun."

That's how it started. Before long they were taking the place apart. They turned over chairs and tables, threw books and papers on the floor, and wrote stuff on the chalkboards. Someone drew a mustache on the picture of the President.

"Hey, give us some help, Manolo," Ray Higley said.

"No!" said Manolo. He thought what they

were doing was crazy, and when someone put a big blob of thick desk paste in the tropical fish tank, he began to worry. *"Ay!"* he shouted. *"Es tonto! Matará a los pescados!"* The one who did this is stupid, he was saying. It will kill the fish. In six months Manolo had learned to speak English quite well, but when he was excited his words often came tumbling out in Spanish.

"Cops!" somebody yelled.

Manolo looked. Two policemen were getting out of a squad car, just outside the playground fence. While one headed for the front door, the other stood guard with his hand near his holster. Someone must have seen the boys breaking in.

"We're trapped!"

"We gotta get out of here!"

"I'm splitting!"

"Hide, you guys!"

They didn't have a chance. The officer burst into the room. Then he started rounding up the boys and herding them into a corner.

"You, with your arm in the fish tank—move! Into the corner!" The officer was talk-

ing to Manolo, who was trying to clear out the paste.

Manolo tried to explain what he was doing, but he was too scared to find words, even in Spanish.

"Move, I said," the officer ordered, and Manolo scurried to join the others in the corner.

The officer flipped on his walkie-talkie. "Jack," he said, "I've grabbed some vandals in here and I need some help. Come in by the front door."

"How many are there?" the voice on the radio asked.

"Five. They're not dangerous. You can park your gun."

"I read you, Hank."

The other officer came inside. He began taking down their names and writing out citations. "Bring these citations to the Hall of Justice," he said as he handed them out. "It tells you when, right there on the fourth line. And be sure to bring a parent or your guardian. Understand?"

Then the officers took notes on the damage and made the boys show how they had broken in. After that they ushered them down the hall and out the front door.

Outside, Manolo read his citation. His hearing was Friday at 4:00 P.M., Hall of Justice, Room 302. Six days to figure out what to do, six days to worry.

Walking home, Manolo felt as if he were moving toward the edge of a cliff on a dark night. He was just plain scared. At lunch, his aunt gave him his favorite North American food—hamburger on a toasted bun. He couldn't eat it. His stomach felt as if he had chewed up a baseball and was trying to digest it.

"What's the matter, Manolo? Aunt Carola asked.

"I'm not very hungry."

She felt his forehead and gave him a glass of milk and some graham crackers. That meant she thought he had an upset stomach. Manolo just sipped a little milk and nibbled the corner of one cracker. He was worried and afraid. At the hearing, what would they ask him? Would anyone believe that he was trying to save the fish? He wouldn't even ask his Aunt Carola to believe it. Even if she did and tried to tell the police what had happened, they would say either that she was foolish or that she was telling a lie to protect her nephew.

The first time Manolo had ever seen his Aunt Carola was when she had met him at the airport, six months ago. He remembered the day he first came into his aunt's home. She showed him his room and talked to him while he unpacked his things.

"I'm sorry I can't be here in the afternoons, when you come home from school," she told him. "I have to work. Here is the address and the telephone number of where I work, in case you need me or want to talk to me. It is a shop where ladies come to have their hair done."

Manolo soon began to think himself very lucky for a boy who could not live with his own parents. Aunt Carola's large, dark eyes and dark hair, her softness and warmth, made him think of his mother. When his aunt was happy, she hummed the same little songs his mother did. Although at times she seemed sad, she was never mean.

"You are very good to me, Aunt Carola," Manolo told her one day not long after he had come to live with her.

"Do you like your new clothes?" she asked him.

"I like them very much. I thank you."

Soon after he had arrived in the United States, she had noticed that the clothes he was wearing were not quite the same as those of his schoolmates. She took him downtown on a Saturday afternoon and let him pick out new ones. She also lengthened his trousers when they grew too short. Although the food she gave him was not always what he had been used to in Chile, he liked it and knew it was making him grow tall. She let him earn spending money by emptying the garbage and doing other jobs around the house. She never spoke sharply to him, but she was strict. She made him take showers and keep his room neat, and insisted that he always be on time for meals. She was happy when he got a good report card, but when he didn't, she only urged him to try harder. "For the sake of your mother and father," she would say.

"I will try," Manolo promised. "But sometimes I don't understand so well what the teacher is saying."

"It is hard," his aunt agreed. "But it will get easier. You will see."

Manolo had telephoned his aunt just once, one day when he was lonely. Another time, when he went downtown to buy some batteries, he found the beauty parlor where she worked and decided to go inside and see her.

She was glad to see him and introduced him to everyone in the shop—the customers and the people who worked there. "This is my nephew, Manolo, from Santiago, Chile," she told them. "He is living with me until things get better in his own country."

When all the ladies greeted him at once, he did not know what to say and felt embarrassed. But he was proud of his aunt because he could see that she was in charge of the shop and that everyone there respected her.

By Monday the school break-in had become like a terrible dream that would leave him for a while, then return again and again, filling him with dread and making his skin feel cold and clammy under his clothes. He wished he could suddenly be back home in Chile, four thousand miles from the Hall of Justice.

"Yes, you, Manolo Blanco!" It was his teacher. "Is something the matter, Manolo? You look a million miles away this morning. Please pay attention."

"I'm sorry, Miss West. Will you say the question again, please?" It had been that way all day for Manolo in school.

That evening he carried the fear with him to his Little League game. He was supposed to be playing right field for the Ed's Car Wash team, but he couldn't pay attention to the game. Suddenly voices broke into his thoughts.

"Manolo! Heads up!"

"Watch it, Manolo!"

"Get under it! Get under it!" That was Mr. Harris, the manager. Everyone was yelling at him.

Manolo looked up to see a long line drive sailing in his direction. He covered his face with his hands and ducked his head. The ball whistled past his ear, thudded to earth behind him, and rolled toward the fence. By the time

he had recovered it and thrown home, Lyons Real Estate had scored two runs.

"For Pete's sake, Manny! Stop dreaming!" the manager shouted. The whole team was on his back.

Before the game was over he had struck out three times and dropped an easy fly. He was in disgrace with the manager, the team, and a number of noisy parents in the bleachers.

If only this were soccer, he would show them some stuff. He would show these Yanquis how to play a real game, the best in the world. No standing around on the field waiting for something to happen. No feeling hot and prickly in a flannel uniform. No sitting on the bench half the time, waiting to bat. No heckling the other pitcher.

In soccer you had no breath left for heckling. You ran all the time, until your lungs almost burst. After a game you were tired, but you felt happy. In soccer you could feel like a championship player wearing only shorts and a shirt, and you could run like the wind. No heavy uniform holding you back. If a kid missed a shot or had the ball stolen, it was no crime. Another chance to make a big play came along in a few seconds. In Little League boys sometimes went home crying because they had missed a fly or struck out, and they knew how angry their parents would be. Soccer was different. Soccer was nothing but fun. And because Manolo had played that hard-running game since he was very small, he felt stronger, swifter, more agile than most kids in his class.

Little League—why was he in it? "Try out for it," his friend Don Wilson had said. "What can you lose?"

So Manolo had joined the Ed's Car Wash team and soon learned how to catch a fly and swing a bat. He was only fair at fielding and batting, but he was a fast runner, and so very soon he was the best base stealer in the league. He had to admit that he liked to hear the yells and cheers when he stole a base. At those times he almost would forget soccer—but not quite. Standing out there in right field, he still dreamed about it, and sometimes he kicked at a candy wrapper as if a soccer ball were right there. That Monday evening just dreaming about playing in a real game, picturing himself booming a ball in for a score, was almost enough to make him forget his trouble.

As Manolo walked home from the game he had caused Car Wash to lose against Lyons Real Estate, he was deep in thought about the Hall of Justice and what was going to happen to him there only four days from today. He hardly noticed the man walking a few yards in front of him—until the man made a surprising move. He suddenly shortened his stride, then broke into a little jog. What he did next, Manolo would never have expected—not here, anyway. Ten feet ahead an empty beer can stood upright, close to the curb. The man ran forward, placed his left foot beside the can but a little behind it, followed through with his right toe, and lofted the can neatly over a car parked by the curb. It all took less than ten seconds, but it told Manolo everything he needed to know. The way the man ran to the empty can, the way he kicked it, there could be no mistake. Great excitement filled Manolo Blanco—and great happiness.

19

He ran ahead and came up beside the man, who now was walking in a perfectly normal way. "Mister . . ." Manolo said shyly.

Surprised, the man looked at him and slowed down.

"Please, can I ask you a question?" Manolo said. "Are you a soccer player?"

The man stopped and studied Manolo closely. With equal curiosity, Manolo returned his gaze. Manolo decided that the man was neither young nor old—maybe a little younger than Manolo's father. He had light-brown hair and blue eyes. Compared to Manolo, this man was pale, a regular Anglo. He was tall but not heavy, and he looked strong. "Yes, I used to play," the man said. "Why do you ask?"

Manolo understood that the man knew exactly why he had asked, but he told him anyway. "The way you booted that can, I could tell."

The man looked pleased and proud. "Are you a soccer player?" he asked.

Now it was Manolo's turn to feel big. The way the man said the words made him feel like someone playing for his town, maybe even for his country, in a World Cup match.

"I used to be," said Manolo. "Where I used to live. Here all I can play is baseball. Only little kids play some kind of soccer game here. But it is not real soccer."

"I know how you feel," said the man. "I played some soccer in college. I always think I'll look for some league to play in, but I never do. Just too busy, I guess."

"Are there soccer leagues in the U.S.A.?"

"Oh, yes. Over in San Francisco. There are a lot of good players here from other countries. Yugoslavs, French, Chinese, British, and a few Americans who played in college."

"No one from Latin American countries?" Manolo asked.

"From Latin America, of course," the man answered. "Mostly, in fact. I guess I take that for granted."

"The best are from Latin America," Manolo stated. He had no doubt about that.

"You're absolutely right—Pelé, for instance," the man agreed.

"Have you got a dry cleaning store or something like that?"

"No. Why?"

"Not any business at all? Not some kind of store or hamburger place? A car wash, maybe?"

"No," the man said. "I just work at a job."

Manolo was disappointed. "I thought maybe you could sponsor a soccer team, if you had a business. The name could be on our shirts for advertising. In Little League, I play for Ed's Car Wash."

The man looked thoughtful. They walked along together for a short distance, then he said, "You played in a soccer league in your country?"

"I played center half for the Lobos. That was our school team. We played against five other school teams. Last year we were the champions."

"They start you young down there," the man said.

"Like baseball here."

"Where are you from?"

"I come from Chile."

"Did you move here with your parents?"

"No. They were arrested. They did nothing wrong. They were against the government."

"Of course—I understand," the man said.

23

"I hope things will soon be a lot better in your country. Do you hear from your parents?"

"Sometimes."

"Who are you living with here?"

"I live with my aunt."

"I see." They walked a little farther without talking. The man seemed to be thinking. Finally he turned to Manolo and said, "My name is Fred. What's yours?" He put out his hand and Manolo shook it.

"My name is Manolo."

"Manolo, how'd you like to kick a ball around with me?"

"You have a soccer ball?"

"That's right. Official International Regulation—genuine stretch cowhide. Would you like that?"

"Yes. I would like that a lot."

"Good. Meet me at the high school football field tomorrow at three."

"I will do that."

"Tomorrow's my day off. We can practice shooting through the goalposts. It's not as good as a cage, but it's better than nothing."

"Thank you. I will be there."

"I'll say good-bye now, Manolo. This is

where I have to pick up my car." They were coming to the Apex garage. "Nice to have met you, Manolo. See you tomorrow." Again he stuck out his hand. It was a big hand, very strong.

"Same here," said Manolo and let him feel that his own hand was strong, too, for his size. He walked home that evening feeling happy and forgetting for a little while the heavy weight that hung over his head. Tomorrow afternoon he was going to feel his foot slam against a real soccer ball. He could hardly wait.

But all the next day in school the worry kept returning, to make a cold nest for itself at the bottom of his stomach. Sooner or later he would have to tell his aunt and give her the piece of paper that said they must go to the Hall of Justice. Then what would happen? Would they take him away from his aunt and put him in Juvenile Hall? Would they make his aunt help pay for the damage in the school? Would it be a lot of money? How could he ever escape from this terrible trouble?

During recess Arnold Driscoll ran past him

shouting, "Send me a card from Juvey!" He meant Juvenile Hall.

Then another kid came up to him and said, "Wow, I heard you got busted." Manolo said nothing, but just walked away. Now he was sure that everyone was looking at him and saying that he had been arrested for breaking in.

The worst was when his friend Don Wilson came up to him and began to say, "Manolo, is it true that—?"

"Yes!" Manolo snapped. "Who told you?"

"Stevey told me. Bill Spender told him." Bill Spender was the boy who had pried open the window and let them in.

"I think that guy is proud to be in trouble," Manolo said.

"I guess he must be," Don agreed. "It isn't his first time."

"He should not talk so much," Manolo said unhappily. Now everyone knew that he, Manolo, a boy who had come from a foreign country, was already breaking the law in the U.S.A. He was miserable and ashamed. At that moment he wouldn't have cared if an earthquake

cracked open the playground and swallowed him up.

Paying attention in class today was harder than ever. Manolo's thoughts darted back and forth between the Hall of Justice and the high school football field. He thought of his new friend, Fred, and of how today he would get his foot on a soccer ball for the first time since leaving home. He hoped the ball would be pumped up to full presure. He hoped his friend would not forget to come. He wished it was time for school to let out.

When school was finally over, Manolo ran all the way to the field. Fred was there, dribbling the ball and taking shots at the goal, the way soccer players do before a game. As Manolo came through the east gate, Fred booted one in his direction. It was a high one, and Manolo caught it on the volley, not letting it hit the ground, connecting solidly with the instep of his right foot. Sure enough, it was a heavy regulation ball that made a beautiful *boom* when he kicked it. His high clearing shot landed almost at the man's feet. In a real game, Fred should have trapped it dead and dribbled it down toward the goal. But he missed the trap. Maybe Anglos were never such good players, or maybe he was just out of practice. That must be it. The ball bounced past him and he chased it. Stopping it finally, he passed it back to Manolo. Not a bad kick. Manolo dribbled it up to Fred, faked to the left, tapped it between his feet and dribbled in for an easy shot between the goalposts. It felt great to be controlling a soccer ball again.

"You weren't exaggerating when you told me you'd played soccer," Fred said. "You're really good."

"You kick very well," Manolo said politely.

"Thank you, but I know the difference. I think the kids in Chile must play in their sleep. It's in their blood."

"Like baseball here," said Manolo. "Down there, everywhere you go you see kids kicking, playing soccer. Always kicking—anything, even if they have no ball. Even a stone." Remembering how it was, he showed off a little. He rolled the ball up on his instep to get it in the air and kept it up there, juggling it from one foot to the other in short, straight-up kicks. Then he sent one high, jumped to meet it with his head, sending it high again.

As it came down, he caught it neatly on one knee, then the other, and dropped it dead at the man's feet.

"Fantastic!" Fred said. "You can really make that ball sit up and beg. What a shame there isn't a team here for you to play on. I'd really like to watch that."

"I would like that, too."

They fooled around some more, running up and down the field dribbling, passing the ball back and forth, and shooting between the goalposts as they got in range. Part of the time Manolo defended the goal. Usually he stole the ball away from Fred, but once or twice he let him get past for an easy shot. Then they did it the other way around, with Manolo attacking.

"Show me in slow motion, Manolo, exactly what happens when your foot strikes the ball," Fred asked. "Obviously you're doing something right that I am doing wrong, the way your shots bang in there. I want to see just how you hold your foot."

Manolo showed him slowly, and Fred tried it, but his shots were no better than before.

"Keep practicing," Manolo advised him.

30

After a while, his friend was out of breath and damp with sweat. Hardly able to talk, he said, "I've had it. I thought I was in good shape. I'd better quit before I fall on my face." He caught his breath a little, then added, "For a Little League baseball player, you've got pretty good wind, young fellow. How do you do it?"

"After the games, I run around the field a lot of times. It makes me feel strong."

"Very fine. Very fine." He was still having trouble catching his breath. As Manolo stood there resting one foot on the ball and looking as if he would like to go on playing, Fred said suddenly, "If more kids got really tired once in a while, they'd be better off, and so would this town. So would the taxpayers," he added.

"I feel good when I'm tired," Manolo said. He wondered what Fred meant. Why did he say that soccer would be good for the town? Manolo had his own reason for believing it would. "In Chile, every town has a soccer team," he said. "A good team brings great honor to the town. But if the children do not play when they are young, then they do not grow up to play well for their town team.

Maybe a soccer league could be started in this town for the kids? Then someday this town could play those in San Francisco?"

"A whole soccer league?" the man said thoughtfully.

"At first maybe only two teams. More teams later." Manolo's mind was racing ahead at a great rate.

"Could be. Could be," said the man. He, too, seemed to be thinking, and Manolo began to have some hope that this might happen, all because he had seen this man kicking a beer can over some parked cars. Even if Fred had no hamburger place or car wash, he could sponsor a team. Soccer had no expensive uniforms to buy. There was no reason he couldn't do it, and that way he could come out and kick the ball around a little, even if he was too old to play. Any team would allow a sponsor to do that.

"Well, it was fun. I enjoyed it and I thank you," Fred said picking up his jacket. "Let's do it again sometime."

"Okay," Manolo said. "When?" he asked, wondering if Fred really meant it. Sometime could mean never.

34

"Soon. I'll tell you what—phone me at my office next week, Monday or Tuesday." He wrote down his telephone number in a little notebook and tore out the page. "Here," he said. "A lady will probably answer. Ask for Fred. I'll expect your call. Good-bye, Manolo. See you soon. *Hasta la vista,*" he added in Spanish. He was saying good-bye.

"Ah! You speak Spanish?"

"*Poco*—a little. Remember to call me."

Fred left by the north gate of the field, carrying the ball, and Manolo left by the east gate. He wondered if ever again in his life he would play in a real soccer game, running, running, running until his lungs felt on fire, yet wishing that the game would never end.

Manolo reached home a little after five. This was the day he would have to show his aunt the citation. She had to arrange to leave the shop early, on Friday, to go with him to the Hall of Justice. He must tell her tonight. He went to his room and took the citation from the book where he had hidden it. Touching it as if it might burn his hands, he thought of what he should say to his aunt. Should he speak in English or Spanish?

35

When he heard her come in, it was just ten to six. He decided to wait a little while before he went downstairs. Should he tell her now or wait until after dinner?

When he got downstairs, she already was standing at the kitchen sink starting dinner, as she often did just as soon as she got home from work.

"Hi, Aunt Carola," he said. He had left the citation upstairs—he had decided to tell her later. She did not turn around or say a word to him. She just continued whatever she was doing at the sink.

"Aunt Carola, I'm here."

Still she did not turn around, but she stopped what she had been doing with her hands. Manolo stood by the refrigerator, looking at her back. The refrigerator switched on and sounded very loud in the silence of the kitchen.

Slowly, then, his aunt turned around and looked at him. Her eyes were darker and deeper than he had ever seen them. Sadder, too.

"Hello, Aunt Carola."

36

"Tell me, please, what happened Saturday morning." Her voice was low and quiet.

"What happened?" He was so surprised that all he could do was repeat Aunt Carola's words.

"What Mrs. Zimmer told me. She said her boy told her. I told her it must be a lie. It's a lie, isn't it, Manolo?"

This was the worst thing that could have happened. Why couldn't he have told her right away? Now it looked as if he were trying to get out of it, hide it. What could he say?

"I was going to tell you right after dinner," he said. "I was going to get the citation. It is in my room. It says I must go to the Hall of Justice on Friday and you must come with me."

"It is not a lie, then."

"It is not a lie." He waited, wishing she would hit him, at least yell at him, be angry. But all she did was look sad. His aunt was hurt, and Manolo knew it was because she loved him and was disappointed.

He went to his room and came back with the citation. "This says we must go the the Hall of Justice Friday afternoon at four o'clock. Aunt Carola, please, I'll never do it again." Manolo wanted to tell her how it had really happened, how he had tried to save the fish and had done no damage in the school but had only gotten a drink. But who would believe that? Maybe his aunt would believe it; but if she did, who would believe her if she tried to tell them? He did not tell her.

She read the citation, then folded it and put it in her handbag and went back to peeling the carrots. All that Manolo could hope now was that she would not cry.

The citation said Room 302, Hall of Justice, April 27th, 4:00 P.M. They got off the bus and walked one block up the hill to the big, new, three-story building. Manolo felt as if his shoes had lead soles two inches thick. His feet did not want to move up that little hill even one step. What would happen to him inside that building?

Yesterday, when he had asked Bill Spender what they do to you at the Hall of Justice, all Bill said was, "Man, you'll find out."

On the door of Room 302, a sign said WALK IN. Manolo followed his aunt through the door, into a small room. She handed the citation to a woman seated at a desk, who looked at it and said, "Please be seated. Detective Paulsen will be with you shortly."

Manolo did not understand. He thought the whole crime had been solved right there at the school when everyone had confessed and given his name. What more did the police need to find out? Did they discover more damage later, after the arrest? This was the worst part yet, sitting there waiting to be grilled by a detective.

A buzzer on the woman's desk sounded. She picked up the phone, listened, and said, "Yes, sir." Then she got up, opened the door to another room, and showed them in. As the door closed behind them, the click of the latch sounded to Manolo like a heavy iron bolt.

Manolo looked at the man seated behind a large desk, reading some papers. He had on a blue uniform with gold buttons and two gold marks on his sleeves. He was wearing glasses. A sign on his desk said DETECTIVE PAULSEN. Then the man looked up, and Manolo could not believe what his eyes saw. Even though the man was wearing glasses and a police uniform, Manolo would have known him anywhere.

Now the detective looked at Manolo again. He looked at him for a long time, then said, "Well!" Then he added, "So!"

He read the citation, then spent a long time studying a paper on his desk. Finally, he stood up and said to Manolo's aunt, "Mrs. Blanco . . . ?"

"No," she said. "Mrs. Ortega. I am the aunt."

"Of course. Of course."

"His parents sent him to live in the United States. I am responsible for him. I don't know how this happened. He is a good boy."

Manolo thought: Yes, she would have believed me.

"Please sit down," Detective Paulsen said. "Let me explain that our city police department tries to keep boys out of the county justice system—Juvenile Hall and all that—if we possibly can. Especially first offenders. Usually a talk with the parents or with a guardian is all that's needed. They usually straighten things out with the boy or girl, and that's all there is to it. Unless, of course, the parents

41

need some straightening out themselves."

"I understand," Manolo's aunt said. "Manolo has always been a good boy. What can I do?"

"I am puzzled myself," the detective said. He looked straight at Manolo and said, "Manolo and I are friends." Then, looking at Manolo's aunt, he said, "Did you know that?"

Her eyes grew wider and darker and deeper than ever. She looked at Detective Paulsen and she looked at Manolo, completely puzzled.

"What Manolo did—what the citation and the report say he did," the detective went on, "surprises me, too. Manolo is a boy who knows how to get tired. He is a soccer player. He is a runner. Boys like that don't often get into trouble. That is what I happen to believe. If I am mistaken about this, then I am very disappointed."

Ah, no, Manolo thought. Now two people are disappointed in me—my aunt and my friend.

"I'm disappointed," the detective continued, "because right now we're planning to give more boys a chance to get tired, get rid of all that unused energy that gets them into trouble, drives them to destroy property. Now I wonder—will it all be a waste of time? Won't it do any good?" He picked up a cardboard sign that was lying on his desk and held it so they could read it. The picture showed a boy kicking a soccer ball. The words said . . .

SOCCER

The Police Athletic Association will sponsor a junior soccer league for boys and girls in the elementary schools above third grade. All wishing to play, leave your names with your teachers.

Manolo felt like a bomb with a lighted fuse. Five seconds passed, then, *"No hice nada!"* he exploded. *"Solo queria beber el agua! Estaba sacando la pasta de la piscina cuando llegó la policía,"* he continued. *"Ellos pensaron que yo estaba metiendo la pasta en la piscina."* There! The bomb had burst, and now he did not care. Let them believe him or not. He had told the truth. All he had done was try to clean out the tropical fish tank.

"Manolo! Is this true? Speak in English!" his aunt exclaimed, turning a helpless look at Detective Paulsen.

"That's all right. I understand," the detective said. "He saved the fish. He did no damage. He only wanted a drink of water. In this job I have to know a little more than English." He was standing up now beside his desk. He was holding the citation. Very slowly he closed his big fist—with the citation in it—then opened his hand wide and let the crumpled paper fall to the floor. Without saying one word, in English or Spanish, he had told them clearly, *Aha! I knew there must be an explanation and I am very glad.* Then, in plain English, out loud, he said, "This makes it a different ball game, I'm glad to say."

Manolo was not sure what he meant by that, but it did not matter—he liked the way it sounded.

Aunt Carola wiped her eyes with a tissue from her handbag. With a flick of his right toe, Detective Paulsen had kicked the crumpled citation neatly into the wastebasket beside his desk. "I suppose you'll come out for soccer," he said to Manolo.

"Yes," Manolo said. A heavy weight had been lifted from his body, and he felt like kicking a ball so high it would never come down.

"But sometimes, Manolo, can we still kick a ball around, just you and I, for practice?"

"I'll call you, Monday or Tuesday," Manolo promised.

"Don't forget," the detective said, and politely walked with them to the door and held it open.

Walking down the hill to the bus, Manolo felt hungry. "Can we have a hamburger on a bun for dinner tonight?" he asked.

His aunt turned toward him. She was smiling softly, and her eyes were shining. "Yes," she said. "As many as you like."

Manolo could tell that she was happy now, and he was thinking about the letter he would write to his parents and big brother.

Dear Mom, Dad, and Raoul,

I have a new friend. His name is Fred. He is a soccer player and a Detective of the Police. Here is what happened. Last Saturday morning . . .

Suddenly Manolo realized that he was thinking English words, not Spanish. Should he write his letter in English? Why not? He had seen his big brother read American magazines. His brother would understand the letter. Would it be showing off a little to write in English? Maybe so, but Manolo didn't care. Let them see that he was learning something in America. They would be proud, too. He continued the letter in his head. When he got home, he would write it down.

. . . some kids were playing in the schoolyard. We got thirsty, but the drinking fountain was broken. One of the kids opened a window in the school, and we all went in. Some kids began to tear the place apart. Suddenly . . .

In his letter, he would tell them just how it all had happened. It would be a long letter.